SAM
A Special Puppy

written by Rebekah Stion

illustrated by Lorraine Arthur

Library of Congress Catalog Card No. 84-052174

© 1985 The STANDARD PUBLISHING Company, Cincinnati, Ohio.
Division of STANDEX INTERNATIONAL CORPORATION. Printed in U.S.A.

It was the week of Christmas. The noise of
shoppers rushing about filled the air. Every
hour the church bells chimed a Christmas
carol.

In a nearby apartment lived Mr. and Mrs. Harper. The Harpers owned a newspaper business and had to be away from home every day. Their pet, Mistie, a beautiful black dog, watched the home while they were at work. Mistie seemed to be especially happy this Christmas. She was going to be a mother.

On Christmas Eve, Mr. and Mrs. Harper called for Mistie to come and go to bed early. Mistie was extra tired and could hardly step up into her bed. Mrs. Harper gave Mistie a warm hug as she laid a blanket over her. She was hoping Mistie would have her puppies by Christmas morning. That would be a wonderful present for everyone.

Early on Christmas morning, strange little noises woke Mr. and Mrs. Harper. They jumped out of bed and rushed over to Mistie's bed. There, curled up beside Mistie was a beautiful black puppy. Mistie was proud of her Christmas present. She licked Mrs. Harper's hand as she picked up the puppy to love.

Mistie was a good mother and gave her baby the best of care. She gave her puppy lots of milk. She gave him a bath every day. He was a picture of health with his soft, shiny fur.

As the weeks went by, the puppy grew stronger and began to walk around with his mother. The Harpers loved to watch them play together.

Six weeks passed. Everything seemed fine until one day Mistie suddenly became very ill and died. This was a sad time for everybody. The puppy needed someone to take care of him. Mr. and Mrs. Harper were busy in their newspaper business and did not have time to give him the care he needed.

On a farm, outside the city, lived a boy named Dean. Like most boys and girls, Dean wanted a puppy to love.

One night at the family Bible reading, Dean's mother talked about having faith in God.

Dean listened very carefully to his mother. She explained that faith meant to trust and believe God for the right answer to our prayers.

Later that night as Dean knelt beside his bed to say his prayers, he asked God to help him find the right puppy. Dean loved God, and he was going to trust God for the right answer. This gave Dean a happy heart as he closed his eyes to go to sleep.

The next morning Dean whistled a tune as he dressed for school. He was excited about wanting a puppy. He greeted his mother and daddy with a big kiss at breakfast.

"I'm so glad to see you are excited about going to school today," said Mother.

A smile covered Dean's face.

Dean told his parents about his talk with God and how he had asked God to help him find a puppy.

As days turned into weeks Dean did not give up. This was what kept the smile on his face, even when things went wrong.

Then, one night while Dean was watching a TV program, the doorbell rang. He rushed to the door. There stood Aunt Wanda, and in her arms was a little puppy. Dean's heart pounded with excitement as he invited her inside.

Right away Aunt Wanda could see that Dean was extremely happy. He couldn't keep his eyes off the puppy. Dean listened carefully as Aunt Wanda told all about Mr. and Mrs. Harper, Mistie, and the puppy. Dean's eyes filled with tears.

Aunt Wanda looked at Dean's mother and daddy. They nodded.

"Dean, would you like to have the puppy?" Aunt Wanda asked. "Would you take good care of him?"

"Yes, yes!" shouted Dean.

As Dean reached
for the puppy, he
whispered a thank-you
prayer to God.

The puppy licked Dean with his tiny pink tongue, and Dean knew that meant, "I love you."

"I love you too," whispered Dean. "I'm going to take very good care of you, Sam. You're my very special puppy!"